BOY DUMPLINGS

by Ying Chang Compestine

illustrated by

James Yamasaki

Holiday House / New York

Text copyright © 2009 by Ying Chang Compestine
Illustrations copyright © 2009 by James Yamasaki
All Rights Reserved
HOLIDAY HOUSE is registered
in the U.S. Patent and Trademark Office.
Printed and Bound in China
The text typeface is Hiroshige Medium.
The artwork was created with watercolor
and gouache on paper.
www.holidayhouse.com
First Edition
1 3 5 7 9 10 8 6 4 2

Library of Congress Cataloging-in-Publication Data
Compestine, Ying Chang.
Boy dumplings / by Ying Chang Compestine ; illustrated by James Yamasaki. — 1st ed.
p. cm.
Summary: When a hungry ghost threatens
to gobble up a plump little boy, the boy tricks the ghost
by convincing him to prepare an elaborate recipe first.
ISBN-13: 978-0-8234-1955-5
[1. Ghosts—Fiction. 2. Cookery—Fiction. 3. China—Fiction.]
I. Yamasaki, James, ill.
II. Title
PZ7.C73615Boy 2009
[E]—dc22
2006050064

To Vinson,
a boy who makes
the best dumplings
—Y. C. C.

To my mom, dad,
and sister
—J. Y.

In the capital of China, Beijing, there once lived a tall, skinny ghost. He believed that only foolish ghosts worked hard for their meals.

This smart ghost simply strolled through streets at night, where people left him offerings in big buckets.

Then, one night, the offerings stopped.

Days passed, and the ghost became so hungry. He wandered all about, willing to eat almost anything.

That's when he spotted a chubby boy. But as he moved closer, the ghost froze. The boy was carrying a brightly lit rooster lantern! The light made the ghost's knees tremble.

The ghost could hardly believe his luck when the boy's lantern suddenly flickered out. He grabbed him.

"Let me go!" cried the boy. "Oh, pyew! You must be the Garbage-Eating Ghost."

"Garbage!" the ghost roared. "I only eat delectable treats!"

"Like me?" asked the boy.

"Yes!" The ghost giggled.

The ghost carried the boy to his house. Once inside, he fetched a bucket and a pair of chopsticks.

"You're not going to eat me raw, are you?" asked the boy.

"Of course," answered the ghost.
"I know a delicious recipe for boy dumplings," said the boy.
"I love dumplings," cried the ghost. "Give me the recipe!"
So the boy did.

BOY DUMPLINGS

Makes 1,000 dumplings
(one serving for a hungry ghost)

1 chubby boy
10 pounds stinky garlic
50 pounds rotten onions
40 pounds wormy cabbage
1 large bottle soy sauce
1,000 moldy dumpling
wrappers

1. Fill 1 bucket with warm water. Wash boy thoroughly, especially behind ears and between toes.

2. Reserve bath water. Dry boy, massage boy's feet, and let boy nap.

3. Wash vegetables in dirty bath water. Chop and mix remaining ingredients. Gently wake boy with feathers....

"And *then* I chop you up!" The ghost dashed out, barring the door from the outside.

Along the river he raced, in and out of stores, upstairs and downstairs, through restaurants, this way and that. He had never worked this hard before, but he knew the boy dumplings would be worth it.

Finally, he came home carrying all the ingredients.

The ghost picked
up the boy and
prepared to drop him
into the bucket.
"Wait!" shouted
the boy. "Where's
your steamer?"

The ghost dashed out again, running in and out of stores, upstairs and downstairs through restaurants, this way and that.

In the city's biggest restaurant, he found a steamer large enough for 1,000 boy dumplings. Hungrier than ever, he rushed home.

Carefully following the recipe, he washed the boy, paying special attention to his grubby ears and stinky toes. Then he wrapped the boy in a blanket and set him down for a nap. The boy thrust his feet at the ghost. "Rub gently!" he ordered. "It will tenderize them."

It wasn't easy for the ghost to resist taking a bite as he gently massaged the boy's toes, one at a time. The boy fell asleep, but the ghost had no time to rest. He washed the vegetables in the bathwater, then chopped and mixed them.

At last he was ready for the sleeping boy. He tickled the boy's ears with two feathers.

"What do you want?" yelled the boy.

"Time to chop you up!" announced the ghost.

"Not yet! For the best dumplings, you must use fresh springwater for steaming."

The ghost thought for a moment and then dashed out.
Along the river he ran, over and under bridges, this way and
that through narrow alleys. In all of Beijing he could not find
even a drop of springwater!

Then he remembered the clear spring at East Mountain outside the city. Off he ran with a large jar. If he didn't eat soon, he feared that he'd be the first ghost ever to die of hunger.

He quickly set the snoring boy on the cutting board and lifted the cleaver.

Something terrible happened! The roosters crowed, and the first rays of sunlight streamed through the windows. The boy had opened the curtains!

"Aaaaaah!" shrieked the ghost. "I need a dark place to hide! I am *meeeeeelllltttttinnng*."

The boy leaped off the cutting board and held up his rooster lantern. "It's dark in here!"

Instantly, the ghost turned himself into white smoke and swirled into the lantern. The boy lifted up the ghost— trapped in the lantern.

"Now we are going to MY home!" he proclaimed.

The boy's mother was waiting for him.
"Where were you, my dear?" She ran to him.

"I have captured the Garbage-Eating Ghost!"
The boy proudly lifted up the rooster lantern.

"How brave and clever of you!"

All the neighbors came to celebrate and
took turns peering into the lantern. They
brought sesame candy, red bean cakes,
coconut buns, and almond cookies.
The boy's mother cooked up 1,000
Boy-Free Dumplings.

They had a big feast under the
rooster lantern.

To this day, the boy lights the
rooster lantern as soon as the sun
sets so the ghost hasn't had a
chance to escape.

Yet!

AUTHOR'S NOTES

The character of the Garbage-Eating Ghost is my creation. The inspiration for this story came when my son was about nine years old. He was filling out just before another growth spurt. One night he was helping me making dumplings. When I saw his chubby cheeks and arms, I thought that if I was a ghost, I would love to eat dumplings made with a boy like him.

On the fifteenth day of the seventh month of the Chinese calendar, the Ghosts Festival begins. It usually comes in late August or early September by the Western calendar. It is the Chinese Halloween. In some areas the celebration lasts a whole month.

The Chinese believe that during this time the gate that keeps ghosts out of the living world opens and ghosts roam free each night. They visit relatives and friends, and receive gifts and offerings.

When night falls during the Ghosts Festival, people leave offerings of food outside their doors. They toss sweet treats and dumplings out into the street in front of the house so hungry ghosts will not haunt the family.

In traditional lore, the ghosts would melt away in the daylight. They fear roosters because their crowing marks the end of the night when all ghosts must return to the dark underworld.

BOY-FREE DUMPLINGS

(Have an adult help you with the cutting and with cooking the dumplings)

Makes 8 servings

Filling:

10 ounces ground pork or beef

4 cups minced cabbage

1 1/2 cups minced leeks

3 tablespoons dark soy sauce

1 tablespoon sesame oil

1 package square wonton wrappers

2 large carrots, thinly sliced into disks

Combine all the filling ingredients in a large bowl. Mix well.

Moisten edges of wrapper with water; spoon 2 teaspoons of filling into center of each wrapper. Bring all corners to center; pinch together to seal. Place dumplings, seam sides up, on carrot slices.

Steam dumplings, covered, for 10 minutes or until dumpling skins are translucent. Repeat procedure with remaining dumplings. Serve warm with additional soy sauce for dipping.